This Ladybird book

belongs to

biggy Choi

A catalogue record for this book is available from the British Library

Published by Ladybird Books Ltd
27 Wrights Lane London W8 5TZ
A Penguin Company

2 4 6 8 10 9 7 5 3 1

© LADYBIRD BOOKS LTD MM

Printed in Italy

Sweet dreams
Josephine

by Nicola Baxter
illustrated by Eric Smith

Ladybird

Josephine's evenings are full of fun.
She gets bubbly in her bath.
She gets dry in her tiger towel.
She gets cuddled in her cosy bed.
Then she is ready to go to sleep.

First her toes get snoozy.
Then her knees seem sleepy.
Her fingers feel floppy.
She snuggles and she stretches.
Her little eyes close.
And then...

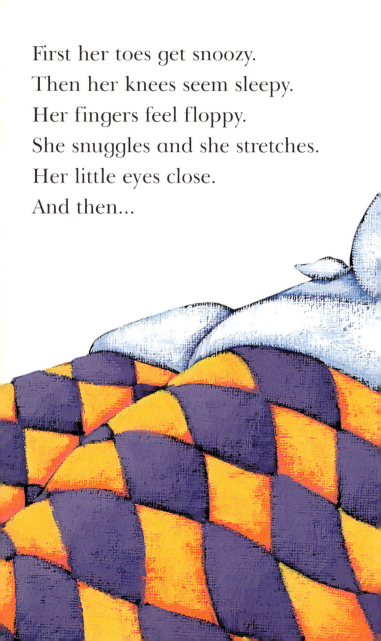

Josephine has the most wonderful dreams…

Dreams where she flies
high in the air.
She soars and she floats,
and all her friends stare.

Flitting past her on every side,
butterflies flutter
and fishes fly,
while bobbing balloons
dance around in the sky.

Sometimes Josephine dreams the strangest of things...

She's walking around
in a tall, gold crown.
People are cheering
all over the town!

She is Queen Josephine!
There never has been
such a beautiful, wonderful,
marvellous queen!

She walks along waving
with her nose in the air...
What a splendidly elegant
royal affair!

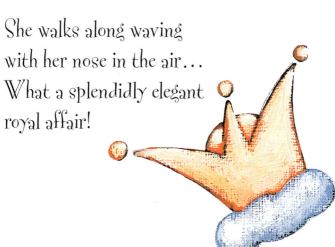

Sometimes Josephine dreams
of bright coloured things…

That her Grandmother sits,
and clickety-clackety knits and knits…
something orange and yellow and
blue and brown and black and purple,
right down to the ground.

It's got green stars and purple dots,
pink circles and red spots!

"It's a scarf… for a giraffe!"
says Gran, with a laugh.

Sometimes Josephine dreams of wild, windy weather…

Of pitter-pattering,
spitter-spattering,
clattering, battering,
rattling rain on the roof.

It beats like a drum,
tum-ti-tum-tum-tum.

It drips and it drops and it suddenly…

stops!

Then everything is quiet.

Sometimes Josephine dreams the most amazing things...

There are lollipops too large to lick,
jellies too giant to jiggle,
toffees too huge to chew,
chocolate too chunky to chomp!

"They're enormous!" says Josephine.

"They're soooo very tall!"

Or could it be that she is small?

Yes, Josephine has the most
wonderful dreams.

But when sunlight slips
over her windowsill,
her toes start to tingle.
She just can't keep still!

She runs down the hall
not making a sound,
to a place where the
very best cuddles are found.

And cuddling seems
even **better** than dreams –
to Josephine!